ADVENTURES OF TOPSY & TIM

Jean and Gareth Adamson

Blackie: London & Glasgow

Adventures of Topsy & Tim First published in 1970

   Topsy & Tim's Monday Book Copyright © 1960
   Topsy & Tim's Tuesday Book Copyright © 1960
   Topsy & Tim at the Football Match © 1963

By Blackie & Son Limited
5 Fitzhardinge Street, London W.1.
Bishopbriggs, Glasgow
ISBN. 0.216.88704.6

Printed in Great Britain by McFarlane & Erskine Limited, Dalkeith.

THIS BOOK BELONGS TO

Jean and Gareth Adamson

BLACKIE: LONDON AND GLASGOW

Blackie & Son, Ltd., 16/18 William IV Street, Charing Cross, London, W.C.2
17 Stanhope Street, Glasgow
Blackie & Son (India) Ltd., Bombay; Blackie & Son (Canada) Ltd., Toronto
216.88657.0

Printed by McFarlane & Erskine Ltd., Edinburgh

When Topsy and Tim looked out of the
window on Monday morning the rain was
pouring down.

The milkman was wearing a big, black, shiny cape.

"Nice weather," called the milkman. "For ducks!"

Two pairs of Wellington boots stood warming near the fire—one pair for Topsy and one pair for Tim.

"I'm not wearing *my* Wellingtons!" said Tim.

(H 365)

Mummy pulled and Topsy pushed—and Topsy had her Wellingtons on, ready to go to school.

"Now you, Tim," said Mummy.

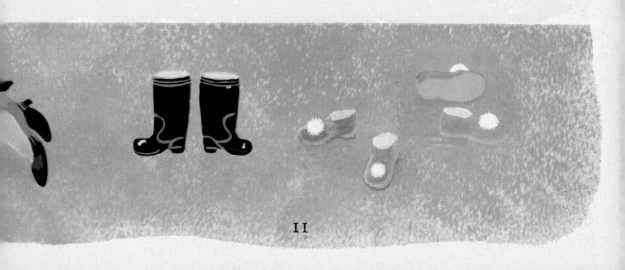

"I don't want my Wellingtons," said Tim. When Mummy scolded him he was very naughty and stamped and shouted, *"I don't want my Wellingtons."*

"It's time that boy learned a lesson," said
Dad. "Let him wear his ordinary shoes."

So when Tim and Topsy started off for school Topsy was wearing her big Wellington boots, but Tim was wearing his ordinary shoes.

Tim could run faster in his ordinary shoes, so he danced in circles round Topsy shouting "Funny boots!"

Tim walked backwards in front of Topsy
and put out his tongue. And then he stepped
right into a deep, deep puddle.

"Yow!" he howled. "My feet are all cold and wet." Topsy walked right through the big puddle and didn't get cold or wet at all.

"Come inside quickly, children," called Miss Maypole, "and change into your dry plimsolls."

"Why ever aren't you wearing your big Wellington boots, Tim?" asked Miss May-pole.

"He wouldn't put them on," laughed Topsy.

"What a silly little boy!" said Miss May-pole. "I shall have to put your wet socks on the radiator to dry."

Tim had to sit on a desk with his bare feet dangling.

When Mummy came to fetch them home she had Tim's Wellingtons in her zip-up bag.

He put them on quickly.

Topsy and Tim plodged through all the big puddles on the way home.

"Good old Wellington boots!" said Tim.

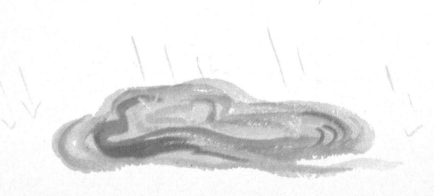

Topsy and Tim's
TUESDAY BOOK

Jean and Gareth Adamson

BLACKIE: LONDON AND GLASGOW

Blackie & Son, 16/18 William IV Street, Charing Cross, London, W.C.2
17 Stanhope Street, Glasgow
Blackie & Son (India) Ltd., Bombay; Blackie & Son (Canada) Ltd., Toronto

Printed by McFarlane & Erskine Ltd., Edinburgh

When Topsy and Tim looked out of
the window for the first time on Tuesday
morning, they saw a big lorry drive on
to the waste land over the road.

"Looks as if they're going to make a start," said the milkman.

"What's 'make a start'?" asked Topsy.

"They're going to build some houses," said the milkman.

"Will the houses be built when we come home from school?" asked Tim.

Dad laughed and said: "No, I don't think they'll be as quick as that!"

Topsy and Tim ran home from school as fast as they could, to see how the builders were getting on with the houses.

They *had* built a sort of house, but it
was small and made of wood.

"Is that a baby house?" asked Topsy.

Tim laughed.

Mummy said: "That's just a shed for
the workmen to keep their tools in."

A big man with red hair and red skin called to them:

"Hello twins! Do you think your Mummy would make our tea for us?"

Topsy and Tim each carried two of the workmen's billy-cans. Each billy-can had some tea-leaves and some condensed milk in the bottom.

Mummy poured hot water in, and they were full of steaming tea.

Topsy and Tim wanted to take the workmen their tea, but the red-haired man came to the back door to fetch it. "Come on, twins," he said, "and meet my mates."

All the builders were sitting on a long plank, eating sandwiches.

They were called Joe and Jim and Fred,
and the red-haired man was Eric. They
were pleased to meet Topsy and Tim.

"Have you ever had a ride in a wheel-barrow?" asked Eric.

He put a clean sack in the bottom of the barrow, and gave first Topsy and then Tim wonderful rides over all the bumps.

Topsy had been a little bit nervous
when she had her ride, but when Tim
came rolling back she wanted another
turn. Mummy came then to take them in
to dinner.

Topsy and Tim watched the workmen
through the window while they ate their
dinner. They waved to them again. Joe
and Jim and Fred weren't always looking,
but Eric waved back every time.

After dinner, Eric called to them:

"I want two strong workmen to help
me shovel some sand."

Mummy found their old sea-side spades.

"I can take bigger spadefuls," boasted Tim.

"I can dig faster," said Topsy.

"You're both doing very nicely," Eric told them.

At four o'clock, Mummy brought them some tea in a real billy-can, and they ate their bread and butter and jam sitting on the workmen's long plank . . . because Topsy and Tim were real workmen!

Topsy and Tim at the
FOOTBALL MATCH

Jean and Gareth Adamson

BLACKIE: LONDON AND GLASGOW

Blackie & Son Ltd., 5 Fitzhardinge Street, London, W.1
Bishopbriggs, Glasgow
Blackie & Son (India) Ltd., Bombay

Printed by McFarlane & Erskine Ltd., Edinburgh

Topsy and Tim's Dad was playing football for his old school one Saturday afternoon, and Topsy and Tim were going to watch the match.

5

Mummy found an old stripey muffler of Dad's, and made it into two mufflers—one for Topsy and one for Tim. She made rosettes for them, too.

"Who wants to be referee?" asked Dad.

"Me," shouted Topsy and Tim together.

"I think Tim shouted louder," said Dad, smiling. He gave Tim a referee's set—a toy watch and a red plastic whistle.

"And here's my old football rattle for you, Topsy," said Dad.

It was a big wooden rattle and made a wonderfully loud noise. Tim wished he had it but still he *was* referee.

Dad had to hurry off then, because he had to be at the football ground first, to change into his football togs.

Although it was a sunny day, Mummy brought out Topsy and Tim's Wellington boots.

"Why are we wearing our Wellingtons?" asked Topsy and Tim.

"You'll see when you get there," said Mummy.

The football ground was very, very muddy.
Topsy and Tim were glad to be wearing
their Wellingtons.
Topsy trod in a deep, sticky puddle and
left one Wellington behind.
"Now you'll have to hop," said Mummy,
laughing.

A 2 (H 569)

But a friend of Dad's stepped out of the crowd and gave Topsy a piggy-back over the mud.
Tim marched in front, blowing his

whistle, and Topsy whizzed her loud rattle. Everyone smiled and made way for them, and they went right to the front of the crowd.

The footballers trotted out of their hut to
start the game.
"There's Dad!" shouted Topsy.
"Dad! Dad!" called Tim.
Dad turned and waved, but he was rather
serious and busy.

The football game was exciting at first.
Then the footballers went to play at the
other end of the field.
Topsy and Tim began to fidget.

Suddenly, the big, muddy ball landed
right at their feet.
"Kick it in, twins! Kick it in!" shouted
the crowd.

Topsy and Tim kicked the ball both at
once. Topsy's Wellington flew off, and
Tim sat down with a bump, but the ball
rolled straight back on to the field. The
crowd clapped and cheered.

Tim was blowing his red plastic whistle as hard as he could, but it was not nearly so noisy as Topsy's rattle. A man in the crowd took a big silver whistle from his pocket. He handed it to Tim and said, "Try this one".

Tim took a deep breath, and blew. "Fffuff" went the big silver whistle. Then he took his finger off the hole and blew again, even harder. The big silver whistle shrilled so loudly that Tim's ears tingled.

The footballers stopped kicking the ball
and looked at the real referee. They
thought he had blown *his* whistle to make
them stop playing.

Then Tim blew the big silver whistle
again, and the footballers looked at *him*.

Some of them laughed but some looked
rather cross.
"Give me that whistle, Tim," said
Mummy, sternly.

The real referee looked at his real watch.
"The game is nearly over now," said
Mummy.
Then the crowd began to shout and wave.
There was a great cheer.
"It's Dad! cried Mummy. "Dad's scored
a goal!"

The real referee blew his whistle. Tim blew his red plastic whistle. Topsy whirled her rattle round and round. The footballers ran off the field to their hut.

"We won!" shouted Topsy and Tim. "We won the football match!"

And they shouted and whistled and rattled all the way home.